The Child's World of
COURAGE

Library of Congress Cataloging in Publication Data

Moncure, Jane Belk.
Courage / Jane Belk Moncure.
p.   cm.
Originally published: 1981.
Summary: Presents various situations that exemplify the nature
of courage.
ISBN 1-56766-296-X (library bound)
1. Courage—Juvenile literature.   [1. Courage.]   I. Title.
BJ1533.C8M66   1996
179'.6—dc20   96-11862
                               CIP
                               AC

The Child's World of
COURAGE

By Jane Belk Moncure • Illustrated by Mechelle Ann

THE CHILD'S WORLD

What is courage?

Getting back on a bicycle after you have fallen off—that's courage.

Letting a doctor give you a shot, even though it stings—that's courage.

Courage is telling a big boy not to tease your little brother.

Practicing a dive off the diving board, even though you didn't do it very well the first time—that's courage. Courage is doing something until you get it right!

Courage is talking things over with Dad when you've done something wrong.

Courage is saying, "I'm sorry," when you fight with your best friend. Courage is making things right again.

18

Telling mother you dried your dirty hands on the clean towel—that's courage.

When you make the last out in a baseball game, courage is not blaming the umpire!

When a friend wants to copy your paper,
courage is saying, "No."

Courage is opening your mouth for the dentist.

Courage is learning to pat the neighbor's big dog—after Mother has said he's friendly.

Courage is trying to be the best kind of person you can be, every day.

Can you think of other ways to show courage?